ßURLINGTON PUBLIC LIP...

Library Regulations

· Any person who lives or works in the Tov...
and residents of towns and cities with w...
...has reciprocal borrowing may take library m...
...he Library upon acquisition of a Burlington lik...

- Borrowed items may be retained for a peri...
...eeks with the exception of reserve books, per...
...nphlets and museum memberships which are
...ìods. No library materials may be renewed.

3. - If library materials are not returned by due c
...er day per item shall be imposed. ...
...em shall be imposed on overdue res
...er day on museum membership.

...ibrary item shall be lost or matei...
...ower to who it is charged shall pay

due on library materials sh...
...n and the money be paid t

...ibrary mate... de
...nes and/...

Be a Super Sleuth!

with

The Case of the Face
at the Window

WOLFGANG ECKE

with **BE A SUPER SLEUTH**

THE CASE OF

THE FACE AT THE WINDOW

Illustrated by Rolf Rettich

Translated from the German
by Stella and Vernon Humphries

Prentice-Hall, Inc.
Englewood Cliffs, NJ

First American edition published 1979
by Prentice-Hall, Inc., Englewood Cliffs, N.J.
Published in Great Britain 1978
by Methuen Children's Books Ltd
11 New Fetter Lane, London EC4P 4EE
Originally published in Germany
by Otto Maier Verlag Ravensburg
Copyright © 1971, 1972 Otto Maier Verlag Ravensburg
in volumes entitled
Der Schloss der Roten Affen,
Der Mann in Schwartz and
Das Gesicht an der Scheibe
This English translation copyright © 1978
Methuen Children's Books Ltd
Printed in Great Britain by
Butler & Tanner Ltd, Frome and London

ISBN 0-13-299115-2

Contents

Contents continued

I • The face at the window

Paul Daimler looked thoughtfully at the letter in his hand. He still felt some misgivings, even anxiety. Should he mail it, or should he tear it up?

Wouldn't it make his nephew Frank believe that Paul was becoming strange in his ways now that he was growing old, that he had started seeing things that weren't there? Once more he read through what he had written:

Dear Frank,

You know you are the only relation I have, the only person I can write to. I'm hoping you can help me. There are strange things going on here, and I'd have gone to the police a long time ago if I hadn't been afraid they'd laugh at me. And it's no laughing matter from my point of view, believe me. I hope you at least will take me

seriously. As I've already said, the whole business is very strange.

It's about four weeks now since it all started.

One evening, I was sitting on the couch in
the living-room, listening to the radio. Suddenly,
outside, I saw a man's face pressed against the
window. At first it gave me such a shock I

couldn't even move. I swear it wasn't a ghost, but a living person, who stared at me and then made a hideous face. I quickly got a flashlight and went out into the garden, but he had disappeared.

The same thing happened again during the next few days, no less than five times. Sometimes he tapped at the window as well, and every time, when I turned to look, this horrible face pressed itself against the glass.

From time to time he left me alone and then, the day before yesterday, something even stranger happened. I was out shopping when I actually saw the man in person. He was in one on of the big stores, making a telephone call, and his sinister face was unmistakable. I could even hear his hame. He was saying: "This is Walters speaking." I didn't have the courage to go up to him and challenge him, but when he caught sight of me he actually raised his hat and called "Good morning!" What does this man Walters want of me? I don't know him nor anyone else named Walters for that matter. And last night he was there again, at the window. I went straight upstairs to bed. What should I do, Frank. Can you help me?

> Your loving uncle,
> Paul

Paul Daimler nodded to himself. Yes, he had described exactly what had happened, no more, no less. He straightened his shoulders, sealed the envelope and took it to the mailbox. On the way, he caught himself twice looking nervously over his shoulder in case he was being followed.

Then Paul Daimler settled down to wait for an answer. A week passed, then another. And he might well have waited a third week, if it had not been for what happened on that particular Sunday....

It had all started peacefully enough. After church he went to lunch at Robert Lesser's house. Lesser, who used to work in the same office before Daimler retired, invited him to lunch regularly once a month. As Lesser put it, at least the lonely widower got a really decent meal once in four weeks.

After lunch the two men played chess for about four hours, and after sitting still for so long they had gone for a long walk. It was, therefore, shortly before eight o'clock that evening when Daimler arrived home.

There was a good movie on television in half an hour, so Paul decided he would watch it and go to bed right after the late news. Then once again....

By now it was ten minutes to eleven, and the weather-map for the following day had just been flashed on the screen. Paul Daimler happened to turn his head. The face! The face was there again, as

10

always, with lips and nose hard against the glass. The mouth was twisted into a repulsive grimace. Daimler stared at it, hypnotized. He wanted to get to his feet, but his limbs felt as heavy as lead. Suddenly the face vanished....

It took quite some time before the old man recovered his self-composure. Had there been a telephone in the house, he would certainly have called the police this time.

With tired legs and heavy arms, he dragged himself upstairs to bed and during a sleepless night he made up his mind. He wouldn't wait any longer for Frank's answer to his letter. Instead he would go and see. him. It was no use putting it off any longer. He would go the next day.

It was already dark when the train pulled in at Breitenberg station, so Paul Daimler took a taxi. But even before the driver could get through the traffic in the busy square in front of the station, the old man felt anxious. Suppose his nephew was away from home? What would he do then?

It was a great relief when he saw that this worry at least had been unnecessary. Frank was in. There was a light burning in his apartment.

He paid the taxi driver and rang the doorbell.

Frank Daimler was an insurance agent going on thirty. "It can't be true!" he exclaimed in

11

astonishment. "My Uncle Paul has come all this way to see me!"

Paul Daimler hugged his nephew affectionately and arm in arm they entered Frank's bachelor apartment.

"This is such a surprise, Uncle Paul. When the bell rang, you were the last person I expected to see. I wondered who on earth it might be. I never dreamed it might be you."

Paul Daimler sat down heavily in an armchair. "If only you'd answered my letter I'd never have imposed on you," he replied.

Frank's face showed utter bewilderment. "A letter? What letter?"

This time it was Daimler's turn to look surprised. "The one I wrote to you, of course."

"When?"

"A good two weeks ago."

"I haven't received any letter from you."

The old man was incredulous. "Are you certain?" he asked.

"One hundred per cent. It so happens I've been at home for the last four weeks, and I've picked up the mail myself every day. But don't look so worried. Now that you're here in person, you can tell me everything face to face instead. Would you like something to eat or drink?"

"I wouldn't say no to a glass of beer - that is, if you have any."

12

Frank sprang to his feet. "Of course there's beer. I'll go and get it."

When Frank had poured out a glass of beer for his uncle he came straight to the point. "Come on, now. Tell me what's the trouble."

The old gentleman gave his nephew a long serious look before replying. "Frank, do you take me for an old fool who's suddenly started seeing things?"

Surprise, incomprehension and finally amusement passed in turn over the young man's face. He looked at his uncle quizzically and grinned. "And I really thought it was something serious," he laughed.

"My question was perfectly serious, Frank," retorted Paul with growing indignation.

"I thought you were pulling my leg," said Frank defensively.

"I'd hardly have made such a long journey just for a practical joke."

Frank made an effort to calm him down. "All right, Uncle Paul. I certainly don't consider you an old fool who's suddenly seeing things. Suppose you tell me what it's all about?"

For a while the old man sat huddled, as if lost in thought. Then he spoke. "For several weeks now I've been seeing the same face, again and again, pressed against the window-pane. Sometimes it's in the kitchen, sometimes in the living-room. Sometimes it scratches or raps on the glass..."

13

"What kind of face is it?" Frank's voice showed his concern and he watched his uncle closely.

"It's a man's face, Frank, a man's face that contorts itself into the most horrible expressions. For weeks now he's been coming almost every day, and it worries me so much that I can't think of anything else. Why does he do it?"

His nephew leaned forward. His voice sounded really sympathetic as he asked: "Wouldn't you like a brandy, Uncle?" And he jumped back, almost in alarm, when the old man shouted: "I knew all along you'd think I'm crazy!"

"No, no Uncle Paul," said Frank reassuringly. "Not at all. Come on, now. Tell me the rest of the story."

Daimler made an angry gesture. "What else is there to tell? I've even seen the guy in a shop. He raised his hat politely and said "Good morning!"

"And why don't you go to the police?"

"They'd never believe me."

"But you don't know they won't if you don't try."

"I don't want to risk them saying I'm out of my mind. And they'd hardly detail a policeman to come to the house and keep watch all day and night, waiting for the face to appear, now would they?"

"All the same, I'd report it if I were you. The police ought to arrest this guy Walters. Isn't that

14

why we pay taxes? The police have a duty to do something for us in return. I for one have to work really hard to earn my salary, and I have to show results too!"

Paul Daimler listened carefully. "That's all very well," he answered. "But suppose this Walters turns out to be a very respectible citizen with witnesses to swear he's the kindest, most decent man in the world? I'd look like a fool!"

For a while there was silence. Then Frank said: "Do go and see the doctor, Uncle. Perhaps there really is something wrong with your nerves. After all, you're alone in the house all day, talking to yourself, I imagine.... Why don't you sell the house and move into an apartment? Or you could lease the place."

Paul Daimler's expression showed how disappointed he was in his nephew. And his voice sounded sad as he said: "I'm tired, Frank. I think it's time for bed."

Next morning, the old man could not be persuaded to stay, although his nephew tried hard to get him to remain for a few days longer. And as he got into the home-bound train Paul Daimler was sure that his only relation considered him a silly old man whose imagination was running away with him and who fancied he was seeing ghosts.

He had no idea that he was quite mistaken in

15

this, that the truth in fact was different - and much nastier. He didn't suspect that his own nephew Frank was actually behind the harassment, that Frank was paying the "face at the window" to haunt his uncle.

Why was Frank doing it? For the time being, that must remain his secret. He may have had an eye on the little house his uncle owned. Who knows?

What was the mistake Frank Daimler made? What proved he was lying? With what remark did he betray that he knew more about the man at the window than he was ready to admit?

2 • The fare-dodger

At a constant high speed, the night express from Amsterdam to Cologne raced along the track. There was something eerie about the lighted windows and flickering lights slipping silently past.

The time was 11:15 P.M.

Hilversum and Utrecht were already far behind and the train rushed on, hurtling through Doorn station. Most of the passengers were either reading or asleep, and only a few peered through windows.

A man in an olive-green trenchcoat was working his way along the corridor of a first-class coach. But every now and then he glanced furtively over his shoulder to make sure no one was watching him.

He looked quickly into each compartment, and at last appeared to have found the one he wanted. Near the window, the two men facing each other in the

corner seats seemed to be sleeping soundly. Two of
the other seats must also have been taken: a pair of
gloves was on one of them and a book on the other;
neither occupant was there at the moment.

The new arrival took off his coat, quietly placed
his suitcase in the rack, and sat down beside one of
the sleeping passengers. The latter's gentle rhythmic
snoring continued undisturbed, even when a couple
of groping fingers touched the grey cloth of his suit.
As soon as the stranger had found what he was
looking for, he immediately switched to another seat.
And not a moment too soon either, for just then
the other two men returned to the compartment.

18

After the briefest exchange of nods, no one took any further notice of the others.

The silence was suddenly broken. "Tickets please!" called a cheerful voice.

The two sleepers were at once awake and five hands dived simultaneously into the appropriate pockets.

The guard had already checked and returned four of the tickets when he addressed himself to the gentleman occupying seat number seventy, who was still fumbling in his pockets and obviously becoming very agitated. "Don't you worry, sir," said the guard quietly. "Just go on looking for your ticket and I'll come back later." With an encouraging smile he left the compartment and went on his way to the next one.

"Perhaps you left it in your overcoat pocket," suggested the passenger in seat number seventy-one opposite.

"No, no. That's impossible. I know I had it here in my jacket."

"You could be mistaken," murmured number seventy-one, and number seventy-three also tried to be helpful: "It's so easy to pull out a ticket by mistake when you go to your pocket for something else. I've often done it myself."

For the umpteenth time, the unfortunate man searched all his pockets. "I can't believe it," he

19

muttered, getting more and more upset. "I'm sure I had it here." And he patted the pocket on his right side, as if he were completely baffled. "Didn't any of you gentlemen notice it, on the floor perhaps?"

"Sorry," said number seventy-three with a shrug. "I only got on at Doorn."

The traveler in seat number seventy-one could only express his regrets too. "I can't help either, I'm afraid. I fell asleep after we pulled out of Amsterdam. What about you?" he asked, turning to seat number sixty-eight.

"I've been in the dining-car most of the time. But don't I remember seeing you with a newspaper in that pocket when we started our trip? Or am I mistaken?"

The man in the corner seat denied this vigorously. "Nothing of the sort," he retorted. "I didn't even buy an evening paper today. In fact, I forgot."

The man in number sixty-nine raised his eyebrows skeptically. "It has occurred to you, I suppose, that you may have forgotten to buy a ticket as well?"

For a moment it looked as if number seventy was going to give his neighbor a punch in the jaw. Then he thought better of it and confined himself to an angry gesture. Five minutes later his shoulders drooped resignedly, and he sighed: "It's simply disappeared, vanished into thin air. I suppose I'll have to pay again. There's nothing else I can do."

20

The guard too came to the same conclusion when, a short time later, he kept his promise and paid a second visit to the compartment. Grinding his teeth in aggravation, the man in seat number seventy handed over the required sum and received in return the usual receipt. His fellow passengers eyed him with disapproval, even contempt. No one has any sympathy for fare-dodgers.

In which seat was the real fare-dodger sitting?

3 • Spot the mistakes

Have you ever wondered what kind of detective *you'd* make? This story contains a number of mistakes: see how many you can find!

In the great entrance hall hung two fine oil-paintings, portraits of the famous Americans, Charles Dickens, who was once President of the United States, and the well-known novelist Abraham Lincoln.

The hall was abuzz with lively excitement, and Inspector Mulligan of Scotland Yard reckoned that the number of those gathered together that evening to celebrate the fiftieth birthday of their host, Sir Arthur Hull, must be at least a hundred. It was the duty of Mulligan and his three junior police officers to keep an eye on things. They had to ensure that nothing unpleasant happened to the assembled guests, who included some of the most distinguished people in the country. He was particularly worried, because there had been an anonymous telephone call earlier in the day, hinting that a notorious pickpocket might well turn up and try to mingle with the crowd.

As soon as Mulligan was informed that all the invited guests had arrived, he called his men together and went over his previous instructions very precisely. "I'm relying on you to keep your eyes peeled," he stressed. "The downstairs rooms open on to terraces on all four sides of the house, and the double doors leading to these terraces are the most likely danger points. Try to behave naturally and make yourselves as inconspicuous as possible. Is everything clear now? Good. Then we'd better spread ourselves out. I want you, Black, to take the north door. Ross will keep an eye on the south side. Forrester, you'd better guard the west, and Pullman, you'll make sure no one tries any nonsense near the east door. Any questions? No? Then take up your positions."

Almost immediately there was a fanfare from the eight-piece orchestra, and a gentleman in a dark blue dinner jacket mounted the stage. In his right hand he held a glass of champagne. "Ladies and gentlemen!" he began. "I know I'm speaking for everyone here if I now raise my glass and ask you to join me in drinking to the health of our excellent host, Sir Arthur. We all wish him well in his new office, and congratulate him heartily on his well-deserved appointment as a minister in Her Majesty's government."

There was a positive storm of applause, everyone drank to Sir Arthur's health and sang "For he's a jolly good fellow." Then there were a few speeches and the evening's entertainment began.

Inspector Mulligan and his men never relaxed their guard. Who was the pickpocket and what was his disguise? How the inspector wished the anonymous letter would prove to be nothing but a hoax!

It was about ten o'clock when the show started. The first act was a magician. He started by asking if twelve of the gentlemen present would lend him their gold pocket-watches. These he placed in his shiny top hat. He then climbed on a chair, lifted one hand as if to give a signal, and all the lights went out. For a few seconds there was an anxious silence. Then a blinding spotlight focused its beam on the magician's chair right in the center of the stage.

An astonished murmur showed that the assembly had indeed been taken by surprise, and Inspector Mulligan broke into a cold sweat. For the magician had disappeared, and in his place a beautiful ballet dancer was balancing gracefully on the chair. This

24

young lady waved her arms and then vanished into the darkness. For the spotlight went out abruptly, and the audience held its breath. Within ten seconds, the four chandeliers blazed into light once more and on the chair stood − the magician!

With a fine flourish, he turned his top hat upside down. It was empty.

"Gentlemen, please," he called above the hum of consternation, "will you be good enough to look and see if all your watches are back in position?" Automatically the fingers of the eleven men concerned dived into their pockets. Yes, all the watches had been safely returned and could be accounted for. There was thunderous applause.

The party was a complete success. And when Inspector Mulligan and his men left the house at four o'clock the following morning, he was very pleased and enormously relieved. Nothing, but nothing, had been stolen.

How many factual mistakes does this story contain, and what are they?

4 • A case for Interpol

The man with the cold black eyes and the pencil-thin moustache strode across the dimly lit tavern looking straight ahead. At the bar he stopped and asked: "Is the Chief in?"

The barely perceptible nod from the old man behind the bar was followed by a movement beneath it, and a key changed hands.

Without so much as a "Thank you" the new arrival made straight for the restroom. One of the three doors inside was inscribed PRIVATE, and it was this one that the key fitted. Behind it stretched a long corridor that ended in a flight of stairs.

Taking these stairs two at a time, the man seemed at first to take no notice of the large oil-paintings on each of the landings. But at the top he paused in front of one picture which had an oriental air to it.

With the flat of his hand he touched the canvas, tapping out a brief but well-marked rhythm, and all at once the painting began to turn as if on a hinge.

The man stepped forward. Immediately the painting, which was also a secret door, closed soundlessly behind him.

He was in a large room, full of cupboards, bookshelves and a number of leather armchairs. On the walls hung large maps of all the continents, and the entire floor was covered with priceless carpets and rugs that muffled even the heaviest footsteps.

At a huge paper-cluttered desk a man was seated. The taut skin of his deeply tanned face was in striking contrast to his shock of snow-white hair. "Back from Ankara already? I didn't expect you till tomorrow at the earliest." His voice was deep, with an icy metallic ring to it.

The other man dropped into a deep leather armchair. "It went much more quickly than we thought possible, Chief. The next consignment is ready."

"What about the quality?"

"Excellent. There's only one thing I'm not happy about. I think Patani is getting . . . well . . . let's say jittery."

The white-haired man put down his gold pen and gave his visitor a searching look. "What do you mean. How is he jittery? Has something happened?" His voice sounded ominous.

28

"He believes there are signs that Interpol has been tipped off. One of his men was picked up in Izmir last week."

"Any stuff on him?"

"No. Only a forged passport. But Patani thinks we ought to dispose of the goods via Aksarai next time. He proposes the twenty-third. If we agree, Dogan can switch the package at the ruins. The method as before ... the one we can trust."

The man at the desk leaned back to look at a wall-map of Europe. His eyes seemed to be drawn to one particular spot. Almost a minute passed before either spoke. Then the white-haired man leaned forward again. "How much is Patani delivering this time?" he asked, no trace of wavering in his voice.

"Seven hundred thousand in one hundred dollar bills."

"Good. Call Dogan and tell him."

Without another word the visitor rose from his chair and picked up the telephone on the desk. With the gold pen he dialed. The ringing tone at the other end could be heard clearly, and then a voice said: "Dogan speaking."

"Hello, Dogan. Ismet here. A new consignment is due on the twenty-third. It will go via Aksarai this time, it's safer. The usual package switch. Using Number Three type packaging. The ten to twelve conducted tour. End of message."

The man who called himself Ismet replaced the receiver. But the Chief rapped out in a tone of command: "And now get me Patani!"

All this happened on Friday the sixteenth. Brooding over Istanbul, the largest city in Turkey, was a layer of stifling, oppressive heat that made breathing difficult even for someone lying still. Not a breath of air came in from the Bosporus to bring a touch of coolness.

One of those who usually suffered in such weather was Miss Joanna Minetti, a special correspondent for a number of West European newspapers. But that Friday afternoon the lady journalist forgot all about the sweltering heat. What had happened was so remarkable that she jumped into her car and drove as fast as she dared to the city center, where she arrived shortly after four o'clock.

At ten minutes past four, she was shown into a room where there were two men. To her surprise, they were both in plain clothes and not in uniform. As she entered, they rose politely and the elder of the two spoke first.

"Good afternoon, Miss. I'm Chief Inspector Kolai, and this is my colleague, Inspector Kemal. You wanted a word with me, I believe."

The woman nodded her assent. "Yes, I'm Joanna Minetti..." she introduced herself, not without a certain hesitation. "You see, I'm a freelance journalist working here in Istanbul. Generally I act quite independently, and if I prefer not to in this particular case it's because I have a hunch it may be too big to tackle by myself . . . and it's probably too 'hot' as well."

She paused a moment and when next she spoke she stressed every word with great precision. "But if you, the police, take action, I want to be present when you move in. That's why I mentioned I'm a journalist."

The two men exchanged a quick, amused glance. Then Kolai spoke. "I must admit you've certainly roused our curiosity. What's it all about, Miss Minetti?"

"First I must ask you a question. Have you a tape-recorder on the premises?"

Kolai nodded and crossed the room to a cupboard, which was crammed with all kinds of equipment. "Here we are," he said, producing a tape-recorder of German make.

Miss Joanna Minetti handed a tape to the officer. "When I'm going to be out," she explained, "I fix an answering machine to my telephone which records messages in case there are any incoming calls for me. But this one has nothing at all to do with me, and I've no idea how it came to be taped. So it's no use asking me. I can't even begin to guess what it's about. Will you play it now — speed 9.5, please."

Chief Inspector Kolai placed the tape on the machine. "Very well then. Surprise us!" he said cheerfully, and pressed the playback key.

A short burst of atmospherics filled the room, to be followed by a high-pitched whistle and finally a voice: ". . . gan speaking."

"Hello, Dogan. Ismet here. A new consignment is due on the twenty-third. It will go via Aksarai this time, it's safer. The usual package switch. Using Number Three type packaging. The ten to twelve conducted tour. . . ."

Immediately after the word "tour" the shrill whistle returned and Kolai switched off.

Both police officers looked very serious all at once, and their change of expression was not lost on Miss Minetti, who felt herself going hot and cold. All the same, she put on a brave face and in as normal a voice as she could muster she asked: "Well, Chief Inspector? Is it 'hot' or isn't it?"

Kolai sounded as serious as he looked. "If I were superstitious, I'd probably say it was Fate, or Kismet as they call it in the Moslem world. But let's just agree that it's a remarkable coincidence. You see, Miss Minetti, Inspector Kemal is from the Interpol Bureau in Ankara. And the information you have just sprung on us fits in with what we were discussing before you arrived like the missing piece of a

32

jigsaw puzzle." Here he turned to Inspector Kemal, inviting him to speak. "Please, Kemal, explain to Miss Minetti what it's all about."

"With pleasure!" said Kemal. "For the past few months, we've been after a gang who are printing and circulating counterfeit American dollar bills. Unfortunately, we've had little success so far. It's true we've picked up one or two of their small fish from time to time. We have an idea, too, that a certain Achmed Patani has a finger in the pie. . . . But that, regrettably, isn't enough. We're looking for the brains behind the organization."

"And you're sure this telephone conversation has something to do with these forgeries?"

"I'm not certain, but I believe it's likely, and I very much hope we're right. A few weeks ago, we arrested one of Patani's men, and that might account for them saying it's safer to operate as far away as Aksarai."

"Where is Aksarai, actually? Isn't it a place where there are some famous historic ruins?"

Kemal nodded. "That's right. It's half way between Kayseri and Konya."

At this point, Chief Inspector Kolai again joined in the discussion. "In fact, you can pretty well take it for granted that the so-called package switch is meant to take place among the ruins."

"That'll be it!" Kemal agreed emphatically. "I

33

don't know of any other site in that region where there are conducted tours. The only difficulty so far is that there are actually three main tourist attractions in the area: the Gayana Tower, the Romchiko Caves, and the Cersa Rocks... We'll have to seal off all three areas."

Joanna Minetti listened, absorbed. "What happens on these tours?" she asked.

"Every couple of hours a minibus arrives at a certain stop to let off visitors and to pick up those who've finished their sightseeing. That is where we must be, ready and waiting."

Miss Minetti nodded. Then, in a voice that refused to take no for an answer, she said firmly: "Then I'll keep the twenty-third free."

The Chief Inspector grinned. "I suppose we could object most strongly, but if you really want to, we won't stop you. However, there is one request, and this we must insist on. There must be nothing published without express permission from us beforehand."

The journalist returned the officer's smile. "It's a rather unwelcome condition, I admit, but I suppose the circumstances justify it. I agree."

"Good. Then I'll let you know tomorrow how we propose to fit you in with our plans."

It was hardly twenty-four hours later that Inspector

Kemal and Joanna Minetti found themselves face to face once more.

"We've been thinking things over very carefully," the Inspector began without delay, "and it's been decided that you'd better be my wife."

Joanna was so surprised that she swallowed hard and stepped back. "But ... but ..." she stammered. "I never dreamed you'd expect me to...."

Kemal had to smile. "I'd be a lucky man to have a wife like you, Miss Minetti, but we'd better get things clear. Our 'marriage' is only for the purposes of next Friday's sightseeing tour. It will look more convincing if we pretend to be a married couple on vacation."

"Sorry if I reacted rather stupidly, Inspector," said the lady, smiling and blushing slightly. "It was only that the idea of finding myself suddenly with a husband seemed so preposterous... But, tell me, which of the three tourist attractions have you decided on?"

"That depends entirely on which our friend chooses. We intend to see that he doesn't even reach the agreed rendezvous. At a certain point, one of our men will take over."

"But why such a roundabout way of doing things?"

"It's quite simple. We want to trace the source of the counterfeit bills. That means we have to find out from the man bringing them where they are made. And once we know who's printing them we'll soon find sufficient evidence to discover who is masterminding the operation and putting the counterfeit bills into circulation."

Miss Minetti happened to glance at the telephone. "Oh, that reminds me. Have you found out yet who made the call that was recorded on my tape?"

"We only know that it was made here in Istanbul. But whether the caller is still in the city is another question."

"There was something else I wanted to know," said Joanna. "What did they mean by a 'package switch' and 'Number Three type packaging'?"

"The package switch means that there'll be two identical containers," he explained, "and by that I mean as alike as two peas. At a pre-arranged spot one man arrives with a perfectly innocent piece of luggage and when no one is looking he quickly exchanges it for one containing the contraband or whatever. 'Number Three type' will tell those concerned exactly what to use: an overnight bag, a sports bag, or even a guitar case. The less striking it is, the better from their point of view. We've no idea what they'll use until we get there."

"I understand. When do we start?"

"We'll meet up at Konya on the twenty-third, but it's a long way from Istanbul so you'd better travel up on the twenty-second, the day before, if you're to be in time for the conducted tour that starts at ten o'clock. Book yourself a room at the Hotel Sasoky. Here you are, I've written it all down for you." And Kemal handed the journalist a piece of paper.

"Thanks. So the idea is that I'll be arriving from Istanbutl, but my so-called husband will be coming from Ankara?"

"Exactly. There's still a lot I have to do, so I'm going back there today. I'll pick you up at the hotel on the morning of the twenty-third."

"Is there anything special you'd like me to wear or be carrying?"

Kemal shook his head. "No, no. I can rely on your good sense." And with a mischievous grin he added: "In any case, I'd never presume to dictate to my wife!"

Everything went as planned. Joanna Minetti set off for Aksarai. Shortly after four in the afternoon on the twenty-second she arrived at Konya, where she parked her car in a garage and took a decrepit old taxi to the Hotel Sasoky.

The room was sparsely furnished. There was a bed, a three-legged stool, a washbasin and two coat-hangers. But the view from the window was all the more beautiful by contrast. Over a distance of twenty-five miles she could see clearly the towering peak of Mount Hassan, nearly ten thousand feet high, at the foot of which tomorrow's meeting was to take place.

Next morning, towards nine o'clock, Joanna Minetti was already waiting outside the hotel when she saw Inspector Kemal coming down the street to meet her. He showed her to his car which was parked near by.

Kemal was a good driver, and as they traveled steadily towards Aksarai he told his companion that he had twenty-four men standing by to make sure they would bring it off.

At twenty to ten they pulled in at the large parking lot. The first stage of their journey was now completed. From here they would have to go by bus.

Kemal scrutinized the twenty or so people present, but so unobtrusively that no one was aware of it. Joanna Minetti on the contrary was enthusiastically taking photographs of everything in sight.

At eight minutes to ten, the bus that ran a shuttle service from the parking lot to the archaeological sites came into view. It was painted bright red, and was equipped with four extra headlights. Seven rather dusty passengers alighted, and twelve of those waiting, not counting Kemal and Miss Minetti, took their seats. The party consisted of three men, five women and four children.

The man from Interpol and the journalist had the back seat to themselves.

"There are only three men," whispered Joanna.

"That makes things much easier for us," answered Kemal, "that is, assuming our man is one of them. I only hope he is."

"One has a black briefcase, another a bulging rucksack, and the third has only a plastic shopping-bag. You can see what's inside it. Two bananas and what looks like a bottle of water."

"You're very observant," said Kemal approvingly. "What else have you noticed?"

"That they're all traveling alone."

"Very good. Anything more?"

"That two of the men are probably Turks and the other is a foreigner. I wonder what the fellow with the rucksack is doing here? He has a coil of rope and a pick too."

Kemal shrugged. "I'm told the Romchiko Caves are a paradise for potholers, and the Cersa Rocks are also worthwhile. Who do you think is Dogan?"

This time it was the journalist who shrugged. "I've no idea. Each of them looks more harmless than the next. But why don't you ask them for their identity papers?"

"Because Dogan is only a cover-up. It's not a name you'll find on anyone's identity card."

"Are you sure?"

"Absolutely certain."

"Have *you* any suspicions?"

"Yes, I have," Kemal answered thoughtfully. "But we'll have to wait to see if they're confirmed."

They went on whispering for some time, safe in the knowledge that the three men, who were all sitting right in front, couldn't possibly overhear what they said. Besides, the women and children chattered so loudly and continuously that they drowned the soft voices of the other two passengers.

At twenty-five minutes past ten, the bus reached the terminal, which was also the weather station for the area. There were three men waiting to conduct the new arrivals on the various guided tours.

And then things began moving fast. The women and children were allowed to go sightseeing, but the three men were whisked off to a room at the back of the weather station, where they were kept under escort for the time being.

Five minutes later, Inspector Kemal had the first of the men brought in to another room which he was using as an office. The excited Joanna Minetti sat at the back, out of the way, but listening eagerly. The man from Interpol was very friendly and polite. "Do sit down, won't you?"

The person addressed was short and dark haired, typical of the inhabitants of the eastern part of the country. "I must protest most strongly!" he shouted angrily, thumping the table with his fist. "I shall complain to the authorities. I'll..." He hesitated and looking sharply at Kemal, then remarked: "One moment, though. You were on the bus just now." Then his eyes lighted on Miss Minetti. "In fact, you were sitting with that young lady there."

"Quite right," replied Kemal calmly. "I'm a police officer and I have to ask you a few questions. It's important, I'm afraid. I see from your papers that you come from Trebizond on the Black Sea."

The man nodded reluctantly. "Yes, that's where I live. I'm a teacher, But I was in Ankara this morning."

"And your name is Alad Shuklu?"

"Yes, it is. And I'm very angry about all this."

"What are you carrying in that bag of yours?"

Shuklu's voice lost none of its hostitlity as he answered: "I'd have thought you could see for yourself. A couple of bananas and a bottle of drinking water. No hand grenades, dynamite or machine guns — nothing."

Kemal was not in the least put out. One could see that the man's unpleasantness simply bounced off and had absolutely no effect on Kemal.

"Does the name Dogan Patani mean anything to you?"

Silence. The man seemed to be thinking hard.

41

"No, nothing. I've never heard of such a person."

"You may go back to the next room now, Mr. Shuklu, but will you please remember that you must not speak to either of the other gentlemen there."

The second man, the one with the briefcase, hurried into the room gesticulating wildly and speaking so fast that Kemal could hardly make out what he was saying. "Now listen to me. Before I say one word, I insist on getting in touch with my consul. Oh, I know you, monsieur. You came with us on the bus a few minutes ago."

"I regret the inconvenience, Monsieur Orelle, but I'm afraid I have no option. You're a French citizen, aren't you?"

Orelle stuck out his chin and glared at the ceiling. But when no one seemed to be impressed by his show of defiance he quickly shifted his uncomfortable position. "I refuse to answer any questions ... except to agree that I'm French."

"May I examine your case?"

"Here it is. All you'll find are a couple of books about your country."

Kemal smiled. "I hope you like our country."

Monsieur Orelle assumed his most ironical expression. He could even wiggle his ears and he did so now. "Until today, I liked it very much. I repeat, until today."

"Why are you here this morning?"

The man hesitated and knit his eyebrows as if the question puzzled him. "Do you mean which of the ruins am I interested in?"

"Yes."

"It was the Gayana Tower I particularly wanted to see."

The inspector handed the case back to the Frenchman. "One last question. Does the name Dogan Patani mean anything to you?"

"Sorry, no. It conveys absolutely nothing to me."

The third and last of the suspects was the man with the coil of rope, the pick and the rucksack. He too seemed indignant at being detained. He flung his rucksack on a chair and his voice had an angry hiss to it. "What's all this cloak and dagger stuff? Why are we being treated like criminals?"

Kemal seemed genuinely concerned. "I do apologize if you've been handled roughly. I gave orders. . ."

"I think its a disgrace that we're being held here without any explanation!" he interrupted.

"We are looking for someone in particular. Your name is Lusin Satran?"

"Right first time. You have my papers and you can actually read. Congratulations!" replied the climber, his voice heavy with sarcasm.

"And where were you proposing to go this morning?"

44

"If you've no objection, I'm going to climb the Cersa Rocks."

"You're very keen on climbing I take it?"

"Yes, I am!" Satran fairly spat out the words and at the same time he stamped the floorboards with his hobnailed boots till they creaked.

"Aren't the Romchiko Caves more interesting?"

The man waved his hand contemptusouly. "I know them inside out!"

"Do you also know the name Dogan Patani?"

The man shook his head emphatically. "No, I've never met either of them."

Inspector Kemal thanked him courteously. "That's all, Mr. Satran. You may go."

Joanna Minetti had been making one or two notes during the questioning. She got up now and went over to Kemal, frowning. "We're no wiser than before. Where does Dogan come into it?"

"Forgive me. I can't even hint at it yet. But Dogan must know already that the game is up."

The young lady looked at the inspector as if she had seen a ghost. "Do you mean he actually *is* one of those three?"

"Correct. And if you want to know who it is, come and watch the famous 'package switch' yourself."

"But which of them is it?" she persisted, her eyes wide with excitement. "The man with the rucksack, the Frenchman with the briefcase, or the teacher with the plastic bag?"

Kemal remained enigmatic. "Come and see."

Which of the three men was really Dogan? Alad Shuklu, the teacher with the plastic shopping bag? Monsieur Orelle, the tourist with the briefcase? Or Lusin Satran, the climber with the rucksack?

5 • The book thief

In two minutes from now, thought Mrs. Kay to herself, I can lock up and go home. But as she turned to go and get her coat, her heart stood still. For there, in the very center of the display at the back of the shop, where pride of place had been given to a large and beautiful volume on Ancient Greece, there was nothing but an empty space. Mrs. Kay's surprise became alarm, and then indignation. Who could have taken this expensive volume, one of the most attractive books in the whole of her shop?

Mrs. Amanda Kay was not the kind of person to stand there wondering. Promptly she made up her mind that the best thing she could do was to go home and telephone Mr. Scott, who would still be at work. For Mr. Scott was not only her tenant, but also a detective, the head of the Investigation

Department of the Safe-and-Sound Insurance Company.

"Now let's get the facts straight, Mrs. Kay," said Mr. Scott half an hour later when he came home from the office. "What happened exactly?"

"I only unpacked the book this afternoon, and I put it out on the counter at the back of the shop where I have a display of big illustrated books, ones on art and history and that kind of thing. There were only two customers in the shop at the time: Mrs. Stubbs and Mr. Lang. As it happens, they are both old customers, people I've known for several years."

"Did they actually buy anything today?" Mr. Scott interrupted.

Amanda Kay nodded. "Yes. Mr. Lang bought a couple of paperbacks, two detective stories, and Mrs. Stubbs bought a book on astrology. I had to find it for her, because she's very short-sighted and she'd forgotten her glasses. Her sight is so bad that she couldn't even tell which coins were which in her hand. I was handing her the parcel when the telephone rang. . ."

Again Mr. Scott interrupted. "Were either of them carrying anything big enough to carry away a book like that without being noticed?"

"Yes, both of them, now you come to mention it. Mrs. Stubbs had a large shopping bag, and Mr.

Lang . . ." Here Mrs. Kay frowned and tried hard to remember. ". . . Mr. Lang had a big briefcase."

"And you discovered the book was missing after they had left?"

"That's right," nodded Mrs. Kay. "And they were my last customers today. No one else came in after they had gone. So it must have been either Mrs. Stubbs or Mr. Lang who took it."

"Which of them left the shop first?"

Again Mrs. Kay had to think. "Mr. Lang left first, I'm pretty sure."

"Good. Now give me their addresses and I'll stop by and hear what they have to say."

Mr. Lang peered suspiciously as he opened his front door the merest crack. "What do you want?" he barked.

"I'd like to speak to you, Mr. Lang. I've come at the request of Mrs. Kay, the lady who keeps the bookshop in King Street."

Albert Lang pointed to a chair. "I suppose you'd better sit down," he said grudgingly. "Is there anything the matter with Mrs. Kay?"

Mr. Scott sat down and came straight to the point. "This afternoon, Mrs. Kay put on display a new and extremely expensive illustrated book. It's priced at $50.00 and now it's disappeared. According to Mrs. Kay, you are a customer of many years' standing."

"I am indeed," he nodded. "And this book has vanished, you say? It wasn't by any chance that fat book on archaeological excavations, was it?"

"The very one. Do you know anything about it?"

There was something in Mr. Scott's voice that made Albert Lang stare at his visitor with growing disbelief. "I see," he said at last. "You've come to find out if I stole it. Of course I didn't. Mrs. Kay should know me better than that. I suggest you call on the lady who was also in the bookshop at the same time. She may know more than I do. And now I'd be much obliged if you'd go." And, very firmly, he escorted Mr. Scott to the door.

Mrs. Stubbs gave Mr. Scott a much friendlier reception. She even offered him a glass of beer. And when he asked her what she knew, she blinked in sheer astonishment. "And am I supposed to have stolen this book? My dear sir, you're very much mistaken." Her voice sank to an excited whisper. "But I noticed something when I was leaving the shop. There was a man at the far side. I was standing several yards away, and he didn't know I could see him. And this fellow was turning the pages of a thick book called *Treasures of Ancient Greece.*"

"Hm," murmured Mr. Scott. "Did you actually see him concealing the book?"

Mrs. Stubbs shook her head. "No, I can't honestly

say I saw him in the act, but all the same. . ."

"Never mind, madam. It doesn't matter. We're nearer a solution now."

The lady breathed a big sigh of relief. "Then at least you don't suspect me any longer!"

"I'm only here to make inquiries, Mrs. Stubbs. That was all Mrs. Kay asked me to do, but I imagine she will get in touch with you again if she needs to. Good night, Mrs. Stubbs."

Half an hour later, Mr. Scott was back at home and able to make a report to his landlady. And she in turned was very pleased that her tenant had suc- ceeded in discovering the truth. And she made up her mind that she would go and have a serious talk with the book thief now that she knew who it was.

Which of the two customers had stolen the book?

6 • The eyewitness

It was eleven minutes past twelve on a fine Saturday night in June. At the far end of Garden Avenue stood two isolated houses dimly lit by a single streetlight.

There was no one about, except for old Mr. Jensen, who was sitting on a bench at the corner of the street, beyond the little pool of light thrown by the lamp. He was enjoying a quiet smoke before turning in for the night. All at once he leaned forward, for someone was strolling down the street and coming in his direction.

Presently the pedestrian reached a big Mercedes, model 220 S, that was parked at the curb. He paused, stepped closer to the car, did something to the window, opened the door and removed various articles from inside. He then disappeared into number

Twenty-one, one of the two houses close by.

The old gentleman was immediately reassured. He knew them all at number Twenty-one, the owner Mrs. Hagen, and all her four tenants, who were students.

The incident had completely slipped his mind until he happened to notice a short item in Tuesday's newspaper:

On Saturday evening, valuable movie camera and other photographic equipment together with an irreplaceable reel of underwater shots were stolen from a private car parked on Garden Avenue. Anyone who can help with information is asked to call the police.

On reading this, Augustus Jensen set out for the nearby police station, and soon he was sitting in an inner office in the presence of Sergeant Henry Herbert.

"It's like this, Sergeant," he explained apologetically. "I couldn't see the person's face because I wasn't wearing my glasses. But I saw everything else. First the chap fiddled a bit with the window, then the door. Finally he took something out of the car and disappeared into number Twenty-one."

"Didn't you suspect it was a thief?"

"No, of course not!" Mr. Jensen was quite indignant. "If I'd thought that I'd have come straight to the police."

"I'm sure you would, Mr. Jensen," said the friendly officer. "Incidentally, do you think it was one of the students?"

"You mean one of Mrs. Hagen's tenants?"

"Exactly."

"Who else could it have been? Mrs. Hagen isn't likely to be running around the streets at midnight, not at her age, and, in any case, I'm sure it was a man."

"Very well. I'll go over there and have a talk with the old lady."

Sergeant Herbert lost no time between making this decision and carrying it out. Exactly an hour later he stood face to face with Mrs. Hagen. He was in luck, for he found that all four students happened to be at home. But Mrs. Hagen was most distressed, and as he climbed the stairs to the first floor he left the lady in tears at the very idea that one of "her boys" could have done such a thing.

It was with Willie Hope, a physics student, that the sergeant began. "I'm Sergeant Herbert from the local police station. There are one or two questions I'd like to ask you, Mr. Hope."

William Hope looked slightly sheepish. "Have I committed a crime or something?" he asked, furrowing his forehead.

"That's what I want to know! On Saturday night, various things were stolen from a car parked in this street. Whoever took them disappeared into this house."

"And I'm supposed to be that guy?"

"I'm trying to find the culprit. What were you doing last Saturday night?"

"I went to the movies. The film was over about ten, and I came straight home to bed."

"Did anything suspicious strike you?"

"No. I didn't hear anything. What was stolen?"

Instead of answering directly, the Sergeant posed another question. "Do you do much photography?"

"A little bit, on occasion. I'm no shutterbug."

"May I look around your room?"

"Of course. But if you're looking for a camera,

you won't find one."

Sergeant Herbert glanced at Willie Hope searchingly before asking: "Why does it have to be a camera I'm looking for?"

The young man shrugged. "It's only that you were asking me about photography, so I thought..."

The police officer nodded curtly and went to the door. "Many thanks for now. I may need to come back again later to see you."

The second student was Martin Singer. He was working on a radio set as the Sergeant entered. "Good morning. Are you Mr. Singer?"

The young man grinned. "I might be. Do you want to convince me I'm not?"

"Hardly," replied Herbert with a smile. "But I need convincing about something else. I'm from the police and I have reason to believe there's a thief in this house."

"How exciting! What am I supposed to have stolen?"

"Last Saturday evening, some photographic equipment was stolen from a parked car. The man was observed but not recognized, unfortunately. However, there is one firm piece of evidence. He definitely entered this house immediately afterwards. What were you doing on Saturday night, Mr. Singer?"

The student didn't need much time to think.

"Several things, if I remember correctly. I wrote an essay, for instance. I answered a few letters. I worked for a while on this radio set I'm building. And at about eleven o'clock I finally went off to bed."

"Do you have any witnesses?"

Singer shook his head. "No, but all the same I can prove that I wasn't the fellow who did it. At the time of the theft I was listening to the radio, that book program, *Midnight to 1:00 am* to be precise."

The Sergeant's hand was already on the door-handle. "I see. Good. Now I'll go and try my luck with your neighbor."

The third student was called Peter Rose, and he had a rather bush beard. His manner was anything but pleasant. "Why have you picked on me?" he asked truculently.

"You haven't seen any photographic equipment in this house during the last few days?"

Peter Rose shook his head decisively, but he still looked annoyed. "Nothing like that."

"What did you do last Saturday evening?"

"I was studying. I always do in the evenings. Actually I was in all day Saturday."

"Do you know anything about cars?"

The student tugged his beard. "I know how to

58

get in and out of a car, and that it has to have gas," he replied sarcastically. "Oh yes. I know it has to be licensed, and that's quite expensive."

"The equipment I mentioned was stolen from a four-door Mercedes sedan. You didn't go for a walk on Saturday night, did you?"

"I really can't remember. Honestly, Sergeant, I haven't the faintest recollection."

The inspector smiled and took his leave. "Oh well. Perhaps the gentleman next door knows a little more."

Sebastian Kaufmann, the fourth tenant, was closing a suitcase as the inspector entered. "Are you going away?" he asked.

"What business is that of yours? Who are you anyway?"

The Sergeant bowed ironically. "My friends call me Henry. Certain of my acquaintances, shall we say, call me Handcuffs Harry. Otherwise, Sergeant Henry Herbert. Satisfied?"

The young man nodded and a slight flush of embarrassment rose to his cheeks. "Thank you, Sergeant. What can I do for you?"

"Did you leave the house on Saturday evening?"

"Last Saturday evening? Let me think. Yes, I did. I was out between eleven o'clock and midnight."

"Think again, Mr. Kaufmann. Wasn't it a little later than that?"

"Not really. I'd been back over a quarter of an hour when someone else came in — at exactly twenty past twelve. I happened to look at my watch."

"And who was it?"

"I've no idea."

"How do you know the time so precisely?"

"I've just told you. I glanced at my watch as the front door slammed."

Sergeant Herbert pointed to two empty cases. "Do you plan to be gone long?"

Kaufmann hesitated. "I'm not going away on vacation, if that's what you think," he said at last, reaching for one of the empty cases. "But before you jump to any more conclusions, let me explain that I'm moving. Oh, it's not because anything's been stolen. It's personal. If you must know, I've had a fight with someone here. And now may I finish my packing, or do you object?"

"Go on with your packing, Mr. Kaufmann. I haven't the slightest objection."

Mrs. Hagen was waiting for the sergeant downstairs. "Have you seen them all, Sergeant? None of them could have done a thing like that, I'm sure.

It's all been a mistake, hasn't it?"

It was obvious that the Sergeant felt rather awkward, but he had to tell the lady the truth. "I'm sorry to disappoint you, Mrs. Hagen, but one of your students is in fact the culprit."

Which of the four students was the thief?

7 • Crossed lines

That Friday morning, Mrs. Bloom was in a greater hurry than ever to get her housework done. The reason for such haste was that she had an appointment at her dressmaker's, and Mrs. Lutter, who had to take Mrs. Bloom's measurements, was always very upset if her customers were late. Mrs. Bloom had to be there at ten o'clock, so she cleaned and dusted and polished as if she were trying to set a new world record.

At half past nine she had finished. Pleased with herself, she cast a keen eye over the gleaming rooms of her apartment and got ready to go out. Then she put on her coat, placed her handbag on the table and went to the telephone to call a cab.

Mrs. Bloom lifted the receiver to her ear and her right forefinger was about to dial the taxi company's number when she hesitated. A man's voice could be distinctly heard. Puzzled, she was about to replace the receiver and start again when she heard a second voice. This voice too could only have been a man's and Mrs. Bloom turned white. She gripped the doorway for support and her knees began to tremble. What she heard was so awful, so dreadful. . .

". . . I wasn't born yesterday, Tony. I've been casing the joint all week."

"Sunday too, Ginger?"

"Sure, Sunday too. But that wouldn't be any good. Too many people around. Monday would be the best day."

"O.K. then. Let's do it on Monday. Have you got it all worked out?"

"I'll say I have! We'll go to the last one, Tony, and when it's finished we'll hide until everyone else has gone. Once the little blonde with the ice-cream has gotten her coat and left, there'll only be the boss sitting at the register, counting all that lovely money. He's always the last to go."

"And how will we get out?"

"As soon as we've convinced the boss that we need Monday's profits more than he does, we'll tie him up politely but efficiently in his chair, and we'll make our get-away through one of the emergency exits. Ha! Ha!"

"Damm it all, Ginger. The poor guy will have to spend all night tied up in that little cubbyhole. Do you think he'll be all right?"

"Don't worry, Tony. He'll survive. The cleaner is sure to find him early on Tuesday morning. Besides, they always come to change the pictures in the display cases on Tuesday mornings. Everything clear?"

"Yeah, perfectly clear. We'll meet as usual, in front of the big poster."

With shaking hands, Mrs. Bloom carefully replaced the receiver and collapsed into an armchair. Five minutes and a glass of brandy later, she felt strong enough to call the police, but her hands were still trembling.

On Monday evening, both Tony and the man with the unlikely name of Ginger were also trembling . . . but with rage. The police were waiting for them.

What do you think was the kind of place that the two villains intended to rob?

8 • The jazz trumpet

Late one Saturday night there was a break-in at the premises of Christiansen & Sons, a big musical instrument shop in Copenhagen. The subsequent investigations made it perfectly clear that this was not the work of a gang, but that a single person must have been responsible.

The culprit had smashed the glass pane of an inconspicuous side door, situated in an unlit yard which was normally used only as a staff entrance. He had forced three cash registers, and had taken 1,225 Kroner from them. Then he had removed the most valuable item from the shop window display, a golden jazz trumpet worth 14,000 Kroner. He had replaced it in the window by an ordinary trumpet of similar design, but had used its case to carry away the stolen instrument when he left the premises.

It was also ascertained that the burglar must have worn gloves, as there were no fingerprints anywhere.

These were the facts of the case. Only twelve hours later, however, the police found unmistakable evidence that whoever had robbed the music shop could only have been someone employed at the grocery warehouse next door. For there, on the top floor, when the three-story building was searched, was found a cardboard box. And hidden in the box were the stolen trumpet and 1,200 Kroner. The remaining 25 Kroner were missing.

After interrogating all the warehouse staff on Monday morning, the officer in charge of the case was able to eliminate everyone except the firm's three junior trainees. One of them must have done it.

So the three youngsters were brought before the magistrate, who was the Chairman of the Juvenile Court, Mr. Sorensen. Their reaction was almost total disbelief when they were handed pencil and paper and told to sit down at different tables, as if they were being asked to take an exam! And their eyes grew wider still when Mr. Sorensen began to speak.

"I've sent for you so that I can find out which of you committed the theft," he began in a firm but friendly voice. "Yes, I'm quite certain that one of you is guilty. You all insist you know nothing about the break-in, nothing about the theft of the trumpet, and nothing about the missing money. Well, you're entitled to say so and until we can prove the contrary you must be considered innocent. All the same, I'm an inquisitive person, and there's something I'd like to know." Here he paused for a moment, and then went on more slowly: "What I wonder is how a completely innocent young man would reconstruct such a burglary from his imagination? How does he think it happened? To put it to the test, I've given you each paper and pencil and I'm allowing you half an hour to write me a brief composition about this theft from the music shop. Imagine you are the burglar. Put yourself in his place. Describe how you got in, what you stole, and how you covered up your traces. Is that clear? Very good. Let me remind you that you have thirty minutes starting now. And don't forget to pur your name at the top of the paper!"

Mr. Sorensen checked the time on his watch, sat down, pulled a newspaper from his pocket and began reading it. Or rather, he only pretended to read. From the corner of his eye he was in fact watching every movement of the three boys, who all hesitated for some time, and then began writing reluctantly, as if they mistrusted the whole business.

68

Exactly half an hour later the magistrate told the boys to stop writing and to hand in their essays. This is what he read:

JIM HANSEN: I broke into the music shop. I'd already had a good look around in the morning to see where I could get in. The yard seemed the best place. There aren't any lights there. So I smashed a window and got in easily. Then I looked for some money. I found some and put it in my pocket. When I'd got enough, I took an expensive trumpet from the window. I moved very quietly so that no one could hear me. I took off my shoes and carried them in my hand. It was very dark, and I had to look out so I didn't bump into things. As soon as I had the money and the trumpet I crept out again.

CARSTEN LAAG: If I wanted to break into the music shop, I'd cut a big hole in the window with a glass cutter. As no one would know it was me, I wouldn't bother with gloves. I could put the trumpet in a case and hide it under my coat. I wouldn't touch the three cash registers. They'd made too much noise. I would also take some records, because they're easy to sell.

ARNE HENDRIKSEN: I broke into the music shop during the night. I got in by the side door, because it wouldn't be noticed there. And it's very dark there as well. I wore gloves so I wouldn't leave any fingerprints. First I collected the money from various drawers, and then I took the trumpet out of the window. It's a real beauty and I'd always fancied it. With the money I found I'll buy myself some real leather gloves with a nice warm lining. I'll wait to sell the trumpet till people have forgotten all about it, and then no one will suspect it's been stolen.

Mr. Sorensen looked up. "Yes, I thought so. Two of you may go, but you and I, my lad" — and here he picked out one of the youngsters — "are going to have a little chat by ourselves. And you're going to tell me exactly why you went shop-breaking."

Which of the three junior trainees gave himself away?

9 • The rehearsal

It was shortly after nine o'clock that the last member of the orchestra arrived at Philharmonia Hall on the morning of the gala concert. It was, as usual, Arnold Stone, the flute-player — he was making it something of a habit to be late for rehearsals. In the doorway he almost collided with a young man wearing a black and yellow sports jacket, who seemed to be in a great hurry. Arnold Stone still found time to say "Good morning" to the friendly doorman Mr. Hart, and although he could hear the string players already tuning up in the first-floor rehearsal room it didn't occur to him to quicken his pace.

Arnold Stone was the kind of person who in spite of good intentions always turned up late for appointments. But as he happened to be a really outstanding flutist, the conductor, Mr. Block, was good enough to overlook his habit of oversleeping. In no time at all Arnold had taken his place and the rehearsal was under way.

At the stroke of twelve, the rehearsal was over. A few moments later, the small cloakroom opposite was crowded with members of the orchestra all talking their heads off and scrambling for their coats. Suddenly there was a sharp, bewildered cry from the oboeist, Max Brand. "My briefcase has disappeared!" he shouted.

Immediately there was total silence. Then the others hastily inspected their various belongings — and with devastating results. Thirty-nine musicians found that money had been taken from their coats, and a few of the missing amounts were quite considerable. Everyone was horrified.

Mr. Block, the conductor, was the only one present to keep his head. "Gentlemen, please, don't panic, I beg you! Just stay where you are for a moment!" he cried, trying to restore order. Then he summoned the custodian, Mr. Corbett. "Will you please get the doorman?" he asked.

A little later, Alfred Hart stood in front of the conductor. When he was told what had happened, the doorman turned pale with shock and groped for a chair.

"Haven't you seen anyone, Mr. Hart?" asked Mr. Block.

The doorman shook his head. "This is terrible, simply terrible," he moaned. "I haven't seen a soul, honestly. I've been downstairs on duty the whole morning." Then

73

his eye caught sight of the flute-player. "You were the last to arrive, weren't you, Mr. Stone?"

The flutist gasped, and for one ugly moment it looked as if he were going to attack the doorman. "Are you suggesting that I . . .?"

"Gentlemen, please, a little self-control!" the conductor intervened.

Stone unclenched his fist and patted his hair nervously. "All it needs now is for you to ask me to turn out my pockets!" Then he remembered something. "Wait a minute, Mr. Hart," he said, pointing a finger at the doorman. "When I arrived this morning I almost collided in the doorway with a young man. He was just

leaving, and in a terrible hurry too. Who was he?"

Mr. Hart frowned and then clapped a hand to his forehead. "Of course," he exclaimed. "Why didn't I think of him before! It could easily have been him. He came from the music publishers to deliver some scores. I wondered why he was so long in the cloakroom, searching among the coats and even picking up people's hats."

"What? He was searching among the coats?" inquired the conductor, appalled.

"Yes. He said he was looking for his scarf, but I realize now what a thin excuse that was!"

The conductor turned to the custodian. Call the police, Mr. Corbett. They'd better find out more about this messenger."

"Certainly, sir. I'll do it right away."

"I'll come with you," announced Arnold Stone, who had recovered his composure. Turning to the others, he said in an offhand voice: "I'm in a hurry. Besides, nothing of mine was stolen. See you all this evening. Goodbye."

Who stole the money from the cloakroom?

10 • Grimble is crazy!

As the instructor, Mr. Grimble, entered the classroom that Friday morning he stopped in his tracks as if rooted to the spot. For there on the blackboard in huge red letters were written the words GRIMBLE IS CRAZY!

Mr. Grimble thought for a moment. This could only have been the work of one of the four boys who had been kept in after school on the previous day. And they were Gerald Fink, Alex White, Michael Cash and Larry Upton.

Mr. Grimble turned the blackboard around so that its unflattering remark could not be seen, and he settled down to mark a pile of books. Half an hour later, when the first of the eleven-year-olds arrived,

Mr. Grimble did not look up.

Then lessons began. The first three periods passed without anything special happening. It was just like any other day. But when the bell rang for recess, the blow fell.

The instructor made the whole class wait while he wrote four names on the board: Fink, White, Cash and Upton. Then he announced: "I want these four to remain behind. The rest of you go out to the playground."

The four boys gathered in front of the blackboard and assumed their most angelic expressions. "One of you has written a most impertinent remark on the other side of the blackboard," he thundered. "Which of you did it?"

The four boys huddled closer, afraid of what was to come.

"Was it you, Gerald?"

Fink shook his head energetically. "No, it wasn't me, sir," he assured the teacher with a most sincere look in his wide eyes.

"What have you to say, Alex?"

"I don't know anything about it, sir," protested Alex, and his ears turned bright red.

Michael Cash had a bright idea. "Perhaps someone broke in during the night," he volunteered as explanation. "And when he saw the bright red chalk lying there. . ."

77

"Is that the best thing you can think of, Cash?" asked the teacher in his most withering tone.

"I only thought..."

"And what about you, Laurence?"

Upton scratched his nose and said rather unconvincingly: "I didn't do it, sir. I don't even know what it says on the board."

Mr. Grimble shook his head. "You really don't know what's written there?" he said incredulously.

"And I don't suppose dear Gerald knows either?"

"No, sir. No idea."

"Michael . . . Alex. . . . Can either of you tell me what it says on the other side of the blackboard?"

"No, sir!" hooted the other two boys in chorus.

Grimble reached forward and his fingers seized an ear. He drew this ear, together with the attached schoolboy, slowly towards him and said in his kindest, softest voice: "Very well. I'll confine myself to punishing the one I know has been telling lies. Run along, you three. You may join your friends in the playground!"

Who was the boy caught telling lies by Mr. Grimble?

11 • The Laxton Motorcycle Grand Prix

There were still thirteen hours to go before the start of the Laxton Grand Prix. This was one of the most important races for motorcycles of all classes, for single machines as well as for those with sidecars.

A long spell of beautiful summer weather had attracted thousands of fans to Laxton, many of whom had pitched their tents or parked their campers within sight of the track. Even now, at eleven o'clock at night, there was an air of excitement about the place. And if you listened hard, you could hear the sound of bathers splashing in the River Laxton, which gave its name to the course.

Fantastic speeds had been recorded during the day's practice runs, and two makes of motorcycles were joint favorites for the team event, Kamaki and Jonaface. Both firms were competing for the first time at the Laxton Grand Prix.

By now, everything was quiet in the pits where the various teams were keeping a strict watch on the superbly tuned machines. The only ones where lights were still burning were those of the Suzuki, the Gran Decco and the Kamaki teams, and also in the Jonaface garage, 200 yards upstream. But even here, by twenty after midnight, all was dark and still.

Tom Hardy of Kamaki sat leaning against a crate, trying to fight his sleepiness. He glanced at his luminous watch. It was exactly three o'clock in the morning, and there was still an hour to go before Mike Sylvester would relieve him, the same Mike who lay beside him on a cot, sleeping peacefully with a faint smile on his face. Tom Hardy kept

81

thinking about Bill, his ten-year-old son, who had had his appendix out the previous day, and was terribly disappointed that he couldn't even watch the race on television. And in his mind, Tom Hardy began writing a letter to him:

Dear Bill,

I'm writing you this letter to keep myself awake. Come to think of it, I've never written to you before. Until now we've always been together, and we could say what we wanted to whenever we liked.

Today was the last practice day and we've come out of it pretty well. As you know, it's our first year here at Laxton. During the trial runs, our team had the second fastest time. I ought to feel pleased about this, and so I do, but what worries me is that the Jonaface machines beat ours and it's their first time here as well. You should have seen the face of their chief mechanic, Steve Miller, as he strutted around afterwards. Of course, I let him know we still had a trick or two up our sleeves. I only hope Meko Tabalis, our star rider, won't let us down. As you can see, Bill, it isn't always easy not to feel jealous; I've seen things happen so often, you know. There's a fellow here on the track who thinks he's hot stuff, when all he's doing is taking unnecessary risks. He's riding for Gran Decco; I can't think of his name at the moment. Actually, I'm awfully tired, Bill, more than ready for bed.

Slowly, gradually, Tom's head drooped forward, and presently his deep even breathing showed that he had fallen asleep.

Ten minutes passed... Suddenly Tom Hardy started. His fatique fell away instantly. There it was again, the same faint metallic click. There was no doubt about it. Someone was interfering with the machines.

Silently Hardy shook Mike Sylvester awake, got softly to his feet and reached for the light-switch. In so doing he stumbled over a can, and this gave the intruder a definite advantage.

By the time the light came on, Tom was just able to recognize a pair of legs disappearing through an airshaft, legs encased in yellow trousers. He dashed outside and when he got to the end of the wall he saw the intruder's shadow reappear, hurrying towards the river. Then the darkness swallowed him up.

Hardy ran back, panting hard. Mike Sylvester was waiting inside and without a word he held out a scrap of yellow material. There was a grim smile on his face, and through clenched teeth he muttered: "Gran Decco!"

Half an hour later, the Kamaki camp was seething with activity. As well as the mechanics, there were the company's competition managers, the race organizers and, at last, the police. Apart from Lieutenant Morris, everyone looked more or less dazed.

The lieutenant's first move was to summon the three mechanics from Gran Decco and to take them to another room. "There can be no doubt that this piece of material comes from a pair of overalls used by your company."

"That's nonsense," replied the chief mechanic, Rodrina, with a sneer. "Do you really believe it's woven exclusively for Gran Decco?"

And his colleague, Ramirez, added angrily: "It's all a frame-up. I wouldn't be surprised if it isn't just a publicity stunt of Kamaki's!"

Rodrina and the third mechanic, Cortez, nodded their agreement. "You can tell there's something fishy going on. Did you know all our spare overalls have been stolen? And without them you can't prove we're involved in any way."

Lieutenant Morris looked at Juan Cortez. "What were you doing at three o'clock?"

The man hesitated. "What do you mean? I was with the others. I wasn't anywhere near the river. I was in the pits."

"And what about you?" asked the lieutenant,

84

turning to Ramirez.

"I was in the pits too. Rodrina is my witness that I didn't set foot outside until all this blew up."

"Is that right, Mr. Rodrina?"

"Yes, it's true."

"So none of you got any sleep? You were all awake?"

There was a moment's silence before Rodrina admitted: "We took turns sleeping."

At this moment the door opened and a slight figure sidled in through the doorway. In his left hand he carried various items of fishing gear, and from his right one dangled a wet bundle. "I was told to give this to a Detective Morris," he said in a grumbling voice.

The lieutenant took the bundle from him and opened it out on the floor. It was a pair of yellow overalls, with a piece torn out of one leg. The scrap Lieutenant Morris held in his hand fitted the tear exactly. "Where did you get this, Mr. . . .?"

"Cockney's the name, Jack Cockney. I just fished it out of the river, behind the pits."

"And when was this?"

The man frowned and thought for a moment. "Sometime between three and three-thirty. I'd arrived a few minutes before and was getting ready to cast my line when this came floating by, caught

85

on a piece of driftwood. It was coming from the direction of the Kamaki garage.

"Are you always up and about so early?" inquired Lieutenant Morris.

At this, Mr. Cockney's face lit up in a broad smile. "It's Nelson I'm after. At least, I've christened it Nelson: the biggest pike you've ever seen. I nearly caught it once, but I was out of luck and it got away."

Juan Cortez jumped to his feet and pointed to the dripping overall. "Do you know what, Lieutenant? It must be the work of the Kamaki outfit. Anyone else would have made sure that overall sank."

The lieutenant smiled a little. "At night, it's almost impossible to see even a floating branch you know."

At that moment, as if on cue, Onega Kamaki himself appeared in the doorway. "Four of our machines have been sabotaged," he said hoarsely, his face flushed with rage. "Have you found the culprit yet, Lieutenant?"

Morris took a deep breath. "I know that someone is telling lies," he answered slowly. "Whether the liar is also the culprit, or if the two are working hand in glove I have yet to establish, Mr. Kamaki. In any event, we're already hot on the trail!"

Who has been telling lies to Lieutenant Morris? And

86

what gave him the clue?

12 • The forged banknote

Joe Gruber, the night manager at the Bear Hotel, put down his pen with an expression of satisfaction and murmured proudly: "Finished!"

That was what he always said whenever he had solved the crossword puzzle in the evening paper. It was a quarter to two in the morning, and that meant he would be on duty for a good five hours yet. And since all the hotel rooms were taken, and all the guests had already checked in, he considered he could safely reckon with a peaceful night ahead, if past experience were anything to go by.

For a moment Joe pondered and then decided to prepare his accounts so that they were ready to hand over to the day manager when the latter arrived at seven o'clock. After that he would re-check the list of early-morning calls and then he could safely settle down and snatch forty winks.

Twenty minutes later, he had sorted out his paperwork and added everything up. All he had to do now was to make sure that he had 631 Marks in the register. He was tidying the banknotes into a neat pile when he gave a start. With a swift movement he directed the beam of the desk-lamp on to the money in his hand and stared at the notes, transfixed. There was no doubt about it. One of the five one hundred Mark notes was noticeably different from the others: the color was several shades darker.

Completely baffled, Joe shook his head. How could he have failed to see it before? Bursting with excitement, he got a magnifying glass from the drawer and scrutinized the note for the watermark... And his hands were trembling with rage when a few moments later he picked up the telephone.

After half an hour of anxious waiting, at last the night-bell rang and Joe Gruber hurried to open the door.

The two gentlemen who followed him inside looked none too pleased at paying a call at such an hour. The shorter of the two, who introduced himself as Inspector Horn, seemed particularly aggrieved at losing his sleep. "This is our technical expert, Dr. Weinberg," he said, introducing his companion and adding enviously with a twist of his eyebrows:

"Scientists can manage with less sleep than us ordinary mortals, so he's wider awake than I am!"

Dr. Weinberg smiled. "Don't worry about disturbing us, Mr. . . . ."

"Gruber's the name, Joe Gruber," said the manager.

"Well, Mr. Gruber, where's the phony note you mentioned?"

The manager produced the five one hundred Mark notes from the register and spread them out on the counter. Without the slightest hesitation, the scientist picked out the darker note and handed it to

Inspector Horn. "From the Dutch outfit, don't you agree?"

The inspector nodded. "Yes, one of the same batch that cropped up in Berlin, I'd say." He turned to the manager. "As you suspected, Mr. Gruber, this is a forgery and not a very good one at that. So you were right to call us. I assume you don't know who planted it on you?"

"I certainly didn't notice it at the time, but it so happens I can limit the number of suspects to three gentlemen, who haven't yet left the hotel."

The inspector could hardly believe his ears. "I hope you're not trying to be funny!"

"No, no — I'm serious. This evening I've taken 631 Marks in cash. Of this fourteen was for various odds and ends like newspapers, stamps and postcards. The rest came from three of the customers who are leaving on the five a.m. train, and so have already paid their bills. Mr. Korner's was 124 Marks, Mr. Baukelius paid 219, and Mr. van Straaten's came to 274 Marks."

Inspector Horn flicked through the duplicates. "And all three gave you one hundred Mark notes when they settled up?"

Gruber confirmed this without hesitation. "As a matter of fact, I've a good memory when it comes to money. Mr. Korner gave me one of the hundreds, plus some small change. The other two gentlemen each handed me two one hundred Mark notes, making up the balance in smaller notes and coins. But what beats me is why the difference in the coloring didn't stare me in the face."

Inspector Horn pointed to one of the three names. "Which room is this man occupying?"

Joe looked at the bill and then at the police officer. "Do you honestly think he's responsible?"

"If the culprit really is one of the three, he must be. Actually, you've been most helpful, Mr. Gruber. It was one remark of yours that gave me the clue. You know, Dr. Weinberg, I won't be at all surprised if we find a few more of these interesting specimens in his luggage. Well, what's his room number?"

"It's 112, Inspector."

Which of the visitors does Inspector Horn think passed the forged one hundred Mark note?

13 • Gentleman Jim

For the third time within a matter of minutes the expensive dark blue sedan swung into Cedar Crescent and purred almost noiselessly past the elegant villas, each of which positively radiated an air of luxury and solid wealth. Behind the handsome wrought-iron railings were well-kept lawns bordered by exotic flowering shrubs. This was the kind of well-to-do residential area where James Baker preferred to work, James Baker who was better known in professional circles as Gentleman Jim.

It was just before eleven o'clock at night.

After the fourth drive past, Baker believed he had found the very house for him. There were no lights on and the garage door was open.

He parked his car on the next road and then proceeded to honor the villa of his choice with an unsolicited visit.

No one would have guessed that the immaculate gentleman in full evening-dress, with a dashing cape, while silk scarf and gloves, was really a highly efficient burglar.

But appearances can be deceptive. Gentleman Jim was an acknowledged expert in his field, even if, from time to time, he had come to know at first hand the inside of a number of prisons throughout Europe.

By eighteen minutes past eleven he had succeeded in forcing an entrance and was standing with head bowed, listening, in the hall of the mansion he had decided to rob. The place seemed to be as empty as he had hoped it would be.

Gentleman Jim got down to work. Systematically he searched every room, beginning with those on the ground floor. His thoroughness was amazing, and his flair for tracing the most rewarding drawers, closets and secret doors was second to none.

Before long his hands were full. He had two necklaces, some cuff-links, a platinum brooch and a purse containing a considerable amount of money. With a bored air he dropped the articles into a pocket. Gentleman Jim was after bigger loot than this.

Finally he came to a room that could only have been a study. And with the assurance of a burglar who knows his craft he at once located the small wall-safe, which was equipped with a high-security lock. As he knew that such a lock is only used where there is something valuable to hide he set to work immediately. His voluminous cape concealed a whole arsenal of precision instruments. But the minutes ticked by without success and Gentleman Jim grew impatient. Never before had he had to spend so much time on a miserable lock, and he became more and more furious with whoever it was who had designed the mechanism.

James Baker wiped a few drops of sweat from his forehead, took off his gloves and placed them on a chair. Again and again he tried and finally, long after midnight, he succeeded at last. With a barely perceptible click the levers yielded. Gentlemen Jim opened the safe door and gave a cry of delight.

Before him, on a bed of red velvet, there glittered an array of jewels whose value could hardly be assessed. He sighed with pleasure and helped himself, stowing away the precious stones inside his pockets as carefully as if he were handling new-laid eggs.

Then he froze in his tracks. He distinctly heard the sound of someone opening the front door. He slipped his flashlight into his cape and darted to the window.

By the time the owner of the house had reached the study James Baker had long since vanished. Only an open window revealed that Gentleman Jim had

been there.

Fifteen minutes later the police were on the spot
and within an hour they were able to arrest the
daring burglar. He had pulled up at a filling-station
for gas, and the attendant, who had been listening to
the radio, had no difficulty at all in recognizing him

from the detailed description given by the police.

Although James Baker denied everything, the Detective Squad could prove his guilt without even trying. One piece of evidence more than any other was of crucial help to them.

What was the piece of evidence overlooked by Gentleman Jim?

14 • True or false?

It was pouring hard on a bleak October morning. Lieutenant Courtney looked at his watch and then stared out of the window. Nine o'clock and raining cats and dogs. Oh, for a cigarette! But his doctor had told him to give up smoking except on special occasions...

Darn it all, thought the lieutenant. Nine o'clock and a morning like this — didn't that make it a special occasion? Yes, it did!

It was after the third puff that he pressed the red button concealed beneath the top of his desk and a policeman poked his head around the door.

"You rang, sir?" he asked.

"Yes. Send in that young man."

The head disappeared and a few moments later a young man was shown in. His appearance was distinctly grubby and his manners seemed equally rough. He didn't wait to be asked to sit down but flopped into a chair. "How much longer must I hang around? I can't mess around here all day!"

The lieutenant took another puff and then said mildly: "Good morning, Mr. Frink."

Adam Frink blinked suspiciously. Then he took a deep breath and began again: "Let me tell you that. . ."

"*I'm* doing the talking here, young man," the

lieutenant interrupted him. "Sergeant Byng tells me that at twenty-five minutes to twelve last night you were caught in the act of . . ." – here he cleared his throat – ". . . of leaving number four Louisa Street by the cellar window. An awkward exit, as you must have discovered. Besides, the house belongs to Mr. Scamp, and although Mr. Scamp may come and go through his own cellar window whenever he chooses, you, young man, are not Mr. Scamp."

After this rather wordy introduction, the police inspector returned to his cigarette, taking little notice of the fact that Frink had jumped up and was shaking his fists. "It's all a mistake, Lieutenant!" he shouted. "I wanted to give the family a surprise. The Scamps are friends of mine. . ."

Lieutenant Courtney seemed absorbed in blowing smoke-rings. Then he said: "Hm." A little later, he said "Hm" again. Another pause, this time followed by: "Tell me, do you always call on your friends through their cellar windows?"

"It was intended as a surprise! I've been trying to explain to the sergeant, but policemen are so thick they only understand words of one syllable."

"Of course, of course. It *is* sometimes difficult to explain things to them! So you wanted to spring a surprise on the Scamps?"

"Exactly. I'd no idea they were away. But when I got there I realized immediately there was no one in, so I turned back right away. I didn't even get as far as the kitchen. That's the truth!"

"The truth?"

"Yes, nothing but the truth."

"An interesting version," said the lieutenant smiling. "I see from your statement that you describe yourself as a student."

"That's right."

"And what exactly are you studying?"

"At the moment I'm on a semester break." Mr. Frink shrugged his shoulders. "Until last semester, I was doing languages."

"Ancient or modern?"

"What d'you mean, ancient or modern? I was talking about foreign languages."

"Of course." Lieutenant Courtney stubbed out his cigarette. "When did you actually discover that the Scamps had gone away?"

"Oh, it was three days ago ... quite by accident. I was talking to someone and he said..."

"Do you remember the time you entered the house?"

From his reaction, one would have thought that Adam Frink was very fussy about getting all the details right. "Of course I know what time it was. Ten o'clock precisely. The church clock was striking the hour. You couldn't help hearing it."

"One last question, Mr. Frink. Sergeant Byng tells

101

me you left the refrigerator door open in the kitchen. Did you?"

Adam Frink shook his head. "Sergeant Byng is mistaken," he exclaimed hotly. "I'm certain I closed it. I remember slamming it."

"Splendid!" said the lieutenant, as if this were just the answer he wanted. "That's all for now. You may go."

"I can go?"

"Yes, back to your cell. Now I know you're just a common burglar. It never pays to tell lies, young man."

"What do you mean, lies?"

"It's quite simple I've caught you lying not merely once but three times. All I can say is that you ought to be ashamed of yourself."

And for the second time that morning, Lieutenant Courtney pressed the red button under his desk.

What were the three lies Adam Frink told?

15 • The man in black

His beard was black and bushy, his glasses had plain gold rims and he wore a drab grey suit. His room was one of the cheaper ones at the Savoyard, a small run-down hotel whose outside plaster was flaking away year by year leaving only a few sound patches.

For half an hour now he had been pacing up and down his room, staring impatiently at the telephone every few minutes. At last, at half past six in the evening, it rang. "Hello!" the bearded man whispered into the mouthpiece.

The voice that answered was no louder than the first speaker's but decidedly less cordial. "Georges, it's me. Just to say that it's OK for tonight. I've prepared things as we arranged. Go to the sixth floor in the staff elevator, and when you get out you'll see a fire extinguisher beside it. The key to 613 is fixed to the back of it with a piece of tape. The things you need are in the cupboard there and the rope-ladder will reach down to the fourth floor. The best time, I'd say, is between two and three. Is everything clear?"

A fleeting smile played around Georges' lips. "Yes, perfectly. And what will you be doing, Pierre, while I'm hard at work?"

"I'm glad to say I'm being sent to Cannes and I won't be back until tomorrow morning. And I hope more than I can say that I'll never set eyes on you again."

A click informed the bearded man that the speaker had hung up. Georges did the same.

That night was moonless. The warm air lay soft as silk over the whole of the French Riviera. In St. Tropez the usual lively parties were still in full swing. The roulette wheels were still spinning in Nice and Monte Carlo. But Antibes had become an oasis of peace and quiet. Along the seafront the few remaining lights in the big hotels were going out one by one.

At exactly twenty past two, a window on the sixth floor of the Hotel Europa was warily pushed open. A man leaned out and looked down, scanning the front of the building. He wore black overalls and a dark mask. After a moment or so his gloved hands began lowering a rope-ladder. With the utmost caution, avoiding any sideways movement, he let out the ladder until it came to rest just above the balcony of a room on the fourth floor.

Again the man leaned out of the window and looked down. For a few seconds he remained there, motionless.

Somewhere in the town a clock struck the half hour. It was a single strident chime that was quickly lost in the sudden roar of a car engine. As if at a signal, the masked figure sprang into action. His body blocked the window opening. But not for long: his feet found the springy rungs and he shinned down the rope-ladder as nimbly as a circus performer.

Once past the open window of Room 513 on the fifth floor he quickly reached the balcony of 413 on the floor below. As he stepped down, he saw that the French windows were wide open and a scarcely perceptible breath of air fluttered the fine muslin curtains at the window.

The masked man held his breath, listening, and he only relaxed when he heard faint snores from within the room. He knew that Signor Ettore Sartoni from Florence was in a deep sleep.

Carefully the intruder eased aside the flimsy curtain.

When he reappeared, a mere four minutes had elapsed. He hardly paused before swinging himself over the balcony and on to the next one, where he repeated his previous performance in even less time. And not only there; his further visits to other accessible bedrooms were not entirely fruitless.

If people don't enjoy breakfast, it's probably because they've slept badly. But if, that next morning, some of the Hotel Europa's guests failed to enjoy their first meal of the day it was not so much because of a restless night as because the discoveries they made on awakening had spoiled their appetite.

Miss Gloria Tucker from Boston, Massachusetts, was the first to burst into the foyer with tears streaming down her face. She seized Monsieur Hector, the manager, by the lapels as she sobbed out her tale of woe.

Hard on her heels came Ettore Sartoni, a jeweler from Florence, followed by a retired general from Bulgaria, Serge Balinoff. The losses they had suffered were enormous, and Monsieur Hector's face grew paler and paler. His small damp hands traveled nervously up and down the seams of his trousers, and his Adam's apple rose and fell with the report of each new disaster. By the time the Aurillacs came tottering out of the elevator, on the point of collapse, the manager could postpone action no longer.

106

Balancing delicately from foot to foot like a flamingo, he teetered his way across the hall to the reception desk and, reaching for the telephone, in a faint voice he asked for the police.

That same afternoon, at about five o'clock, there was a knock at Perry Clifton's door.

Perry Clifton, the famous detective, was spending a holiday at Antibes. He had just returned from a long hot afternoon on the beach and was stretched out comfortably on his bed.

"Come in!" he called, slightly annoyed at being disturbed, but also curious as to the identity of the middle-aged man in a light beige suit who edged into the room with embarrassment.

"Do forgive me, Mr. Clifton. My name is Michel Dumont. I'm sorry to disturb you, but I wonder if you can possibly spare a few moments for a colleague in need of your help?"

Perry Clifton jumped to his feet, amused. "There must be some mistake, Monsieur. I think you've come to the wrong floor."

Michel Dumont was clearly puzzled. "Aren't you Mr. Perry Clifton?"

"I am."

"The detective from London?"

This time it was Perry's turn to look surprised. "Yes, but I didn't think anyone here in Antibes

107

knew about me or what I do."

"If it will put your mind at rest, I'm prepared to reveal the source of my information. A certain Mr. Pickles who often stays here told me who you are."

Perry Clifton jogged his memory. "Pickles? The name certainly rings a bell."

Dumont came to his aid. "He's a big shot in one of the insurance companies in the City."

"Of course, that's it!" exclaimed Clifton. "He has a dog he calls Horatio. In fact, it was a case involving the dog that brought us together."

"Small world, isn't it?"

The Englishman nodded. "You started by asking me if I could spare a moment for a professional colleague. Do I take it then that you're a detective too?"

"Yes, I'm the house detective here at the Europa. And, to tell you the truth, it's a job with more headaches than rewards," said Dumont grimly.

"Oh come, Monsieur Dumont," smiled Perry. "Being here on the Riviera, with the sunshine, white sands, blue skies and even bluer sea — to say nothing of all these charming rich people ... isn't that worth something?"

"These charming rich people, as you call them, are the cause of all the trouble," said Dumont, his face eloquent with meaning.

"I understand. But what is it I can do for you?"

Michel Dumont did not beat around the bush. "I need a hand," he answered, "and there's no one else I can ask."

"But how can I possibly help you?"

"You know about last night, I assume?"

Perry nodded. "I heard that some rooms were burglarized, and when I came in a short time ago I saw that the entrance hall was swarming with policemen."

Ah yes," muttered Dumont. "Our splendid local policemen! Between you and me they're a darned nuisance. What happened last night was that a cat burglar took advantage of the warm night and open doors and windows to drop in on some of our wealthiest clients — and with enormous success from his point of view, it seems. Since ten o'clock this morning the police have been in and out, blithely cross-examining everyone. Your turn will come soon, I imagine, Mr. Clifton."

The French detective walked slowly to the window and looked out. As he turned back to Perry, his voice had a defiant ring to it. "I have to confess that Inspector Mellier and I don't exactly hit it off, and he doesn't think much of me as a detective. Well, I'd like to show him this time that I'm quicker off the mark than he is, and that I can solve the case first."

By now, Perry Clifton, who had been listening

attentively, looked much more eager to co-operate. "So far so good. Only how do you think I can help you? Are there any hard facts to start with?"

The hotel detective beamed with delight. He seized Clifton's hand and shook it warmly. "I knew it!" he exclaimed. "I knew you wouldn't let me down. Of course there are facts and, indeed, there are quite a lot. Some that Mellier knows, and some that only I know."

"Let's begin with the first ones."

"The investigations so far show clearly that the thief was operating between two and three this morning. He let down a rope-ladder from an unused staff bedroom on the sixth floor, that is, from Room 613. We found the ladder in the closet. It was just long enough to reach the fourth floor which, as you probably know, is the only floor with balconies.

"The burglar must have climbed down and landed on the balcony of Suite 413, which is occupied by a certain Signor Ettore Sartoni, a jeweler from Florence. I'm afraid he's about 70,000 Francs the poorer since last night, with losses in both jewelry and cash.

"The next of our guests whom the villain honored with a visit was in the next suite, a Swiss lady, Frau Treicher. She's said to be extremely wealthy, and owns a few hotels herself. She too lost a considerable sum. On the fifth floor, the American young lady, Miss Tucker, was the first victim. According to her, the burglar made off with a jewel case whose contents were worth 120,000 Francs.

"Next to her is a retired Bulgarian general who has just sold his memoirs for a handsome sum. He came here telling everyone that he intended to spend it all, and now it looks as though he'll have no problems in that respect. It's all been taken, together with the necessary tax receipts from the French authorities."

"Anyone else?"

"Oh yes. There are the Aurillacs from Paris in the suite next to the General's. Madame's jewelry and Monsieur's wallet are both missing."

"Quite a greedy fellow, isn't he?" interjected Perry Clifton.

"You can say that again! The last victim was Mr. Stan Simpson from Texas. He's in the room below Frau Treicher's. Mr. Simpson puts his losses at around 20,000 Dollars in cash, and he says a diamond-studded cigarette case has also disappeared."

Perry Clifton shook his head. "I can never understand why rich people carry all that valuable stuff around with them. One question, though, Monsieur Dumont. If only the fourth-floor rooms have balconies, how could the man come and go so easily in and out of the fifth-floor windows?"

"There's a wide ledge that runs all around the building just below the fifth-floor windows. It wouldn't present any difficulty for an expert cat burglar."

"So, altogether, six clients have been affected." Perry Clifton summed up the position so far. "And three of them have rooms or suites on the fifth floor?"

"Yes. You can imagine the state the management's in. Then along come the police, interfering, rushing about with all the tact of a charging rhinoceros, and still completely in the dark as to who could have done it. It so happens that all the well-known cat burglars who might tackle this kind of job are already safely under lock and key. The culprit might be someone living in the hotel, but it could just as well be a man from outside."

"So much for the facts shared by you and Inspector Mellier. But what else do you have up your sleeve, Monsieur Dumont? Let me see your trump card!"

Although Michel Dumont again looked slightly embarrassed, he quickly recovered his self-composure. "I may not know if the burglar is a resident here or not," he explained eagerly, "but I suspect an accomplice of his has a room in the hotel."

"And is this suspect a man with a name, or is it

112

only a guess?"

"My suspect is called Pierre Bassu. He's an assistant chef and like several of the staff — me too, by the way — he has a room on the sixth floor. Yesterday, quite by chance, I noticed Bassu coming out of Room 613, but he didn't notice me. Now I ask you, Mr. Clifton, what was he doing in that room, which is unoccupied at present?"

"Room 613, eh? That's the one where you said the rope-ladder was found. Yes, you're right. That seems very strange."

"Bassu could certainly have left the rope-ladder there for an accomplice. And I should also mention that this is Bassu's first season on the Europa's staff."

"That in itself wouldn't be grounds for suspicion," commented Perry Clifton thoughtfully.

But Dumont raised his hand. "Let me finish. According to his papers, he used to work at the Hotel Tunese in Paris, but when I tried to check his references . . ."

Clifton leaned forward. "Yes? What was the result?"

"It was most interesting. The Hotel Tunese doesn't exist. There's no such hotel in the whole of the Paris area."

"Well, well. You've already succeeded, Monsieur Dumont. What more do you want? All you have to do is to turn Inspector Mellier loose on this Bassu."

113

"No, no," said the Frenchman, shaking his head, "I don't want a half-baked victory. And that's what it would be if it turns out that Pierre Bassu is no more than a minor accomplice. It can't have been Bassu himself, you see. From yesterday afternoon until this morning, the management had sent him as relief chef to our sister hotel, the Royale in Cannes. To be honest, it was here I hoped I could count on your collaboration, Mr. Clifton. I was going to ask if you couldn't try and get the truth out of Bassu. You see, he knows who I am here and therefore he'll be on his guard against me. I'm dangerous as far as he's concerned, whereas you. . ."

Perry Clifton couldn't help grinning. "In other words, you want me to pretend to Bassu that I'm a fellow crook? But suppose it misfires?"

"As I see it, there are only two alternatives. Either he's involved, in which case he'll own up eventually. Or else he's completely innocent, and then he'll be the first to call for help."

"And I'll find myself in a very tricky situation," commented Clifton.

"I'll be at hand, I assure you. I'll come to your assistance if you need me."

"Very well! When should I call on the gentleman?"

Dumont thought for a moment. "Bassu is off duty between six and eight this evening. He's kind of a lone wolf and he usually spends his free time in his

114

room. I suggest you tackle him then."

It was exactly seven o'clock.

Perry Clifton tapped lightly on the door of Room 642 and waited. He was wearing a hat pulled down over his forehead and dark glasses. In one hand he held a matchstick which he was idly chewing.

"Come in!" said a sleepy voice from the other side of the door. The English detective entered, closed the door softly behind him and leaned against it.

"Evening, Pierre!" he murmured and scowled at the man on the bed.

Pierre Bassu was a thin man of about forty. He got up reluctantly and looked at his visitor with a weary expression, which changed first to one of bewilderment and then to one of rage. "What do you want?" he cried hoarsely.

Perry spat out the match and with one finger he pushed his hat back and replied lazily: "Don't you remember me, Pierre? I'm Tommy from London. You can tell by my accent, can't you? Well?" Clifton did not give the man time to reply, but went on remorselessly: "You've messed things up for me very nicely, I must say. That business with the rope-ladder is my speciality, remember? I'd got it all worked out and I was biding my time. Why else

115

would I be living it up in a posh joint like this?"

There was a menacing edge to his voice, and he stared piercingly at Bassu through his sunglasses.

Bassu swallowed hard and groped for words. When at last he spoke, he was almost incoherent. "It's j...j... just as I thought. You're mis... mis... mistaking me for someone else, sir..."

"Am I really? I'm mixing you up with another fellow?"

"That's right, sir. I didn't have anything to do with this robbery."

"That's a laugh! There's a burglary at the hotel, and our dear friend Pierre has nothing to do with it!"

Again Bassu swallowed. He was in a state of panic and his voice had grown even hoarser than before. "I wasn't even in the hotel last night," he protested.

As Perry took a pace forward, Bassu immediately stepped back, so that the distance between the two men remained the same. The Frenchman eyed the door longingly.

This glance was not lost on Clifton who remarked sarcastically: "It's not very healthy out there on the landing, Pierre. The police are waiting for you. Tell me now..."

Bassu didn't let him finish his sentence. "I'm not afraid of the police," he interrupted with more haste than conviction.

117

"What? Have I really made a mistake?"

"Yes, you have. I told you so right away, sir." replied the man with returning hope.

"Now I'm completely mystified. Just imagine, Pierre. I could have sworn you were the chef I knew in Paris. Why, he's your double."

"It c ... c ... can happen sometimes," stammered Pierre, mentally calculating the distance to the door. But Clifton would not let him off so easily.

"I really took you for a man who did the cooking at the Hotel Tunese ... such a coincidence."

The color drained from Bassu's cheeks. His face was like chalk and he was terrified out of his wits as he slumped back on the bed, while Clifton continued ruthlessly: "Why aren't you working in Paris, these days? You had a comfortable berth at the Tunese."

"How is it you know so much about me?" croaked Bassu, his voice so weak that Perry felt almost sorry for the man. He decided not to prolong the agony.

"Come on, Bassu. I'll give you one more chance. Tell me the name of the cat burglar and I promise to keep your name out of it when I report to Inspector Mellier. Is that O.K.? Out with it!"

Pierre Bassu sat huddled on his bed, and stared in front of him, resigned. His voice was resigned too, almost hopeless. "So you're not a crook. You're from the police. I knew there'd be trouble ... But Georges Bardin had me in the hollow of his hand."

118

"Did he blackmail you?"

"Yes. I'd spent some time in jail and when I came out I couldn't get a job anywhere. No one wanted to employ a chef with a prison record. It was Bardin who got me false papers. And I soon discovered why he was so keen to help me. Suddenly he turned up here in Antibes, and threatened me that he'd tell the management about my past if I didn't fix things for him... What could I do?"

The story Bassu had to tell aroused Clifton's interest. He took off his sunglasses and removed his hat. "I'll try to smooth things out for you. So the thief's name is Georges Bardin. And where can we find him?"

"He has a room at the Savoyard Hotel."

Clifton's hand was already on the door-handle. "Thank you for your valuable assistance, Monsieur Bassu. For the time being, please behave as if nothing has happened."

When Michel Dumont came into the room he was carrying two glasses and a bottle of champagne.

Clifton welcomed him enthusiastically. "From your festive preparations I assume you've landed your fish safely?"

"Yes, indeed, Mr. Clifton. He was arrested fifteen minutes ago. Inspector Mellier has had his nose put

119

out of joint. He bombarded me with questions, but I only smiled and muttered something about having 'various contacts, you know'! By the way, you were quite right. Bardin immediately tried to put the blame on Bassu, as you said he would."

"What will happen to Bassu, poor devil?"

"You needn't feel too worried about him. It's going to be all right. Mellier questioned him, of course, but he's been let off with a caution. And the management here has no objection to his remaining on the staff."

"I'm delighted to hear it. But what about the stolen goods though? Have they all been recovered yet?"

"Yes, I imagine so. Bardin didn't have time to get rid of the goods. We found everything in the false bottom of a trunk in Bardin's room. But what's so amusing about that?"

"I'm trying to imagine the expression on someone's face when it becomes known that the thief has been arrested and the stuff recovered too."

"I don't understand what you're driving at, Mr. Clifton. What expression do you expect?"

"One of shock . . . or even alarm."

"I still don't understand."

"Then I'll explain. Of Bardin's six victims, one will be very scared — the one who was telling a pack of lies."

"Are you saying ...?" Michel Dumont struggled for words. "But that's impossible!"

"No, it isn't. Don't you remember my saying: 'All these charming rich people!'? But it may console you to know that even they sometimes try to defraud insurance companies."

Dumont shook his head, completely lost. "But which of them is it? And how on earth did you find out?"

"Simply from your description of the so-called victims. I'm sure you can work it out for yourself. It's not so difficult. All you have to do is follow the footsteps of the cat burglar! Your very good health, Monsieur Dumont!"

Which of the hotel's guests had made a false statement about being robbed?

Solutions

The face at the window, page 7.

Frank Daimler stated that he had never received his uncle's letter. If that were true, he couldn't have known the name of the "face at the window". Yet he said "The police ought to arrest this guy Walters..." before Paul Daimler had actually mentioned the man's name.

The fare-dodger, page 17.

The real fare-dodger was the man in seat seventy-three. He told the others he had "only got on at Doorn", but the train hadn't stopped there. We are clearly told that "the train rushed on, hurtling through Doorn station".

Spot the mistakes, page 22.

There are seven mistakes of fact in this story:

1 Only one of the two men whose portraits were hanging in the hall was American. Charles Dickens was English;
2 Charles Dickens, the novelist, was never President of the USA;
3 Abraham Lincoln was President of the United States of America, but hardly a well-known novelist;
4 At first the party was supposed to be for Sir Arthur's fiftieth birthday. Later it was said to be in honor of his appointment as a minister;
5 Mulligan brought three officers with him at first, but later he put four men on duty;
6 The "anonymous telephone call" about the pickpocket became an "anonymous letter" later on;
7 The magician collected twelve watches, but only eleven gentlemen checked their pockets afterwards.

A case for Interpol, page 27.

The wanted man was Lusin Satran because he was the only one who knew that Dogan Patani was not the name of one man but that two people were concerned. Besides, he could be detected from the start because of what he was carrying. A plastic bag was quite unsuitable, and a briefcase too obvious. Only the rucksack would have served the purpose.

The book thief, page 47.

It was Mrs. Stubbs who was the thief. How could she have made out the title of a book from a distance of several yards when she was particularly short-sighted and had forgotten her glasses?

The eyewitness, page 53.

The thief was the student named Martin Singer. He betrayed himself with the remark: "At the time of the theft I was listening to the radio, that book program *Midnight to 1:00 am...*" Apart from the eyewitness, only one person could have known that the theft took place within this period of time. And that one person was the thief.

Crossed lines, page 62.

The place they intended to rob could only have been a movie theater.

The jazz trumpet, page 66.

The culprit was Carsten Laag. He gave himself away by revealing that the trumpet was carried away in a case, and that he knew there were three cash registers in the shop. Besides, it was very silly of him to write in the essay almost the exact opposite of what had actually happened.

The rehearsal, page 72.

The thief must have been the doorman, Mr. Hart. If he hadn't left the street entrance all morning, as he pretended, how could he have seen the messenger searching through coats and hats in the first-floor cloakroom?

Grimble is crazy! page 76.

The ear grasped by Mr. Grimble's fingers belonged to Michael Cash. He gave himself away when he showed that he knew the words on the blackboard were written in *red* chalk.

The Laxton Motorcycle Grand Prix, page 80.

The fisherman was telling lies. Anything thrown into

126

a river drifts downstream not upstream. The Jonaface garage was situated 200 yards up-stream from the Kamaki camp, so the bundle must have been thrown in the river near the Jonaface pits and could not possibly have come floating from the direction described by Jack Cockney. The fisherman must have been in the pay of Jonaface, the rival team.

The forged banknote, page 88.

In this case, the culprit can only be Mr. Korner for he was the only one of the three who paid with a *single* one hundred Mark note. Inspector Horn realized this when Joe Gruber remarked: "What beats me is why the difference in the coloring didn't stare me in the face." It would have, if he had been handed two notes together, one a forgery and the other genuine.

Gentleman Jim, page 93.

Even an "expert" crook makes mistakes. Gentleman Jim's error was to forget his white gloves. And in his particular case they were as good as leaving a visiting card with his full name and address. Also, of course, not using his gloves meant he left his fingerprints on the wall-safe.

True or false?, page 98.

Lie 1 Frink stated first that he didn't even know the
       Scamps were away. Then he declared he had
       found this out three days before;
Lie 2 He entered the house at 10 p.m. and was
       arrested at 11:35 p.m. Therefore he did not
       leave again immediately, as he stated;
Lie 3 He maintained the first time that he hadn't
       gotten as far as the kitchen. Later he in-
       sisted that he hadn't left the refrigerator
       door open, but the refrigerator was, of
       course, in the kitchen.

The man in black, page 103.

The visitor who only pretended he'd been robbed
was Mr. Stan Simpson. The burglar could not have
reached his room, since the rope-ladder only ex-
tended as far as the fourth floor. Mr. Simpson's
suite, however, was below Frau Treicher's, that is, on
the third floor. So the burglar could not have
entered his room at all.